# GILLIAN CROSS

# POSH WATSON

## Illustrations by Mike Gordon

WALKER BOOKS

AND SUBSIDIARIES

LONDON • BOSTON • SYDNEY

First published 1995 by
Walker Books Ltd, 87 Vauxhall Walk
London SE11 5HJ

Text © 1995 Gillian Cross
Illustrations © 1995 Mike Gordon

This book has been typeset in Garamond.

Printed in England

British Library Cataloguing in Publication Data
A catalogue record for this book
is available from the British Library.

ISBN 0-7445-4109-3

Books by the same author

*Beware Olga!*
*The Demon Headmaster*
*The Mintyglo Kid*

For older readers

*The Great Elephant Chase*
*Wolf*

# CONTENTS

# CRUMBLE LANE

Crumble Lane School was dull. Not just a bit dull, like other schools, but so dull that even the spiders on the ceilings yawned.

The school uniform was grey, the classrooms were cold and bare, and all the teachers were as dull as dust. Especially Mrs Juniper, the Head. Her voice was so boring that everyone yawned every time she spoke.

The only person who was happy at Crumble Lane was Natalie. That was because she never took any notice of Mrs Juniper. She didn't care about the teachers either, or the classrooms. She spent her whole time sitting with a heap of Maths sheets, working away as hard as she could. She liked Maths better than anything else in the world.

And every time she finished a
sheet, her teacher took it away and
stuck it up on the wall, as a
decoration.

*That's* how boring Crumble Lane
was.

# HOWDY-DOODLE-DO!

One dull Monday morning, Natalie
was tying her grey school tie round
the neck of her grey shirt when
there was a knock on the door.

Natalie opened the door – and
almost fainted.

Outside was a boy in a purple
jacket. He was wearing giant
sunglasses and his hair stuck out all
round his head, in bright yellow
spikes.

He waved his lunch box at her. It was gold, and his initials sparkled in diamonds on the side.

"Hi, I'm Posh Watson," he said, "your new next door neighbour."

Natalie picked up her grey school coat, kissed her dad goodbye and stepped outside. "All right. Follow me," she said.

But Posh wasn't much good at following. For most of the way he was ahead of her, turning cartwheels along the pavement and waving at everyone in grey uniform. By the time they reached the school gates, there were twenty children following, all with their mouths open.

Mrs Juniper was standing in the
playground with the bell in her
hand. When she saw Posh, she
almost dropped it. *Her* mouth fell
open.

Posh cartwheeled straight
up to her.

Hi! I'm Posh Watson. It's great to be here. Fan-doodle-tastic!

"I – er – " Mrs Juniper didn't know what to say. "Good morning."

Posh yawned.

But Mrs Juniper didn't even notice. People always yawned when she spoke.

She rang the bell – and Posh stood on his hands and waggled his feet in her face.

Hoo-doodle-ray. Let's get inside and start the fun!

# COPYING POSH

Natalie had a dreadful day.
Whenever she tried to settle down
with her Maths sheets, people came
up and poked her in the ribs.

All the children knew she was Posh's neighbour, and they thought she knew everything about him. They wouldn't leave her alone – even when she pulled faces and growled at them – because they wanted clothes like his.

By Tuesday, everyone else seemed to be mad too. When Natalie got to school, the playground was full of peculiar clothes.

And everyone was yelling strange words.

Natalie stood and stared. She seemed to be the only person in ordinary school uniform. Everyone else was trying to be Posh Watson. She looked round for the real Posh, to see what he thought about it all.

But he wasn't there. Even when Mrs Juniper came out to ring the bell, there was no sign of him.

Or was there?

Suddenly, a Rolls Royce drew up outside the school and a very strange person stepped out of the back. He was wearing a long cloak and a black hat was pulled down over his hair. He came slinking through the gates and over to Natalie, just as Mrs Juniper rang the bell.

The strange person swept off his hat. It was Posh all right, but he looked quite, quite different.

Natalie blinked. "W-where's your purple jacket? And what about the spikes in your hair?"

"Do me a *favour*." Posh looked at her, crushingly. "Spikes are out. Only bondos have spikes in their hair now."

"B-bondos?" Natalie said.

"That's right." Posh waved a hand scornfully round the playground.

Mrs Juniper rang the bell again, and Posh stalked into school, leaving everyone else muttering behind him.

Natalie sighed. Today was going to be even worse than yesterday. She'd be lucky if she got any work done.

She was right. The moment she sat down in her corner at the back of the class, people began to creep up to her.

Mrs Juniper wasn't very happy, either. When they left school that afternoon, they found a notice stuck up on the school gate.

No purple coats!
No spiked hair!
BY ORDER
J. Juniper

# BOOM-BA-BOOM!

There weren't any purple coats
or spiked hair at school on
Wednesday, but lots of people
came in black cloaks and hats with
feathers. The feathers got tangled
up, and the cloaks kept knocking
things over and catching on
splinters.

Natalie thought it was all Posh's fault. But she couldn't say anything because he wasn't there.

He didn't get to school until playtime. And when he did, he wasn't wearing a black cloak, or a hat with a feather.

He came marching into the
playground in a pair of huge pink
trainers that played trumpet music
whenever he took a step.

And he wouldn't say anything
except:

On Thursday, Posh was there early. When Natalie arrived, he was lying in the middle of the playground doing press-ups, in a T-shirt and a pair of running shorts. He had bare feet.

Natalie glared at him.

"Why aren't you wearing your trumpet-trainers?" she said crossly. "Everyone else is."

Posh jumped up and did a back flip. "Exactly! Musical shoes are glazzed-out."

"Glazzed-out?" Natalie said.

Glazzed right out. They're not whirrabubble.

Natalie groaned. She was having a dreadful week. By that afternoon, she'd done only two and a half Maths sheets, and the teacher didn't put those on the wall. All kinds of other things kept getting stuck up instead.

Whenever Natalie settled down to work, people flicked notes at her and hissed in her ear.

People kept trying to find out
what Posh was going to do *next*, so
that they wouldn't get left behind.
And they all thought Natalie knew,
because she was his neighbour.

She was having a miserable time.
So was Mrs Juniper.

# THIS HAS GOT TO STOP

On Friday morning, Natalie and
Posh walked to school together.
As they reached the gates, someone
pushed a note under Posh's nose.

Natalie looked at him. He was wearing a long earring, with a packet of chewing gum on the end, and a false moustache.

Natalie dragged Posh
up the corridor to Mrs
Juniper's office,
knocked on the
door and pushed
him in. He was still
cross, and he
grabbed hold of her
arm and
pulled her in too.

Mrs Juniper
looked at Posh.
She looked at the
earring and the
chewing gum and
the moustache.
And she frowned.

This has got to **stop**!

42

"The Inspectors are coming on Monday," she said. "Everyone's *got* to wear uniform."

She wrote a new notice.

Then she thought again, and wrote another one.

When she'd done that, she looked severely at Posh. "On Monday, I want to see you in a proper school uniform. Like Natalie."

"Like Natalie?" Posh looked at her and his eyes widened. "You mean – you want me to wear a skirt?"

"Of course not!" Mrs Juniper snapped. "I want you to wear Proper School Uniform. Like – like that." She pointed at last year's school photograph which was stuck up on her wall.

Posh stared at the rows of children in neat, tidy uniform.

"But if you don't wear them, nobody else will," Mrs Juniper said. "There will be terrible trouble when the Inspectors come."

"I don't care about trouble," Posh said. "And I've got a really whizzaceous idea for Monday."

Mrs Juniper looked as if she were going to faint. "But everyone will copy you!"

*Oh, dear!* thought Natalie – and that was when she had her brainwave.

She looked at Mrs Juniper. She looked at Posh. She thought about the Inspectors. Then, in a very small voice, she said, "I've got a *really* whizzaceous idea. If you do what I say, you can both have what you want…"

# THE INSPECTORS

On Monday, Natalie got up early.
She dressed as usual, in her school
uniform – grey skirt, grey shirt, grey
tie. Then she ran downstairs and
phoned Samantha, the school
gossip.

Then she had her breakfast and
walked to school with her fingers
crossed.

At five to nine, the Inspectors arrived in their big black cars. They looked out over the playground. All the children were in neat school uniform. Even Posh Watson.

Natalie went up to them.

Shall I take you into assembly?

The Inspectors nodded, and yawned even harder. Natalie knew just what they were thinking. *This school is even duller than last time we came.* She crossed her fingers again and led them into the hall.

They sat up on the platform,
yawning as the children walked in.
They looked very bored.

When all the children were
sitting down, there was a most
extraordinary noise at the back of
the hall.

TARA-TARA-TARA!
BOOM-BA.
BOOM!

# And in came the teachers!

Every teacher was wearing
something wild and strange and
weird. And
behind them
all, dancing
and prancing up
the middle of
the hall, came
someone Natalie
hardly recognized –
*Mrs Juniper!*
She bounded on to
the stage, beamed at
the Inspectors and
held out her hand.

The Inspectors sat up straight and their eyes opened wide. They weren't yawning any more. And they didn't yawn when Mrs Juniper showed them round the school.

They were too busy looking at
the pictures on the walls.

At the neat, tidy children.

And the wild, weird teachers.

And the amazing, energetic Head
– Mrs Jumping Juniper.

Mrs Jumping Juniper was so
happy she was actually smiling.
She'd got what she wanted at last.

Posh was smiling too. Because *everyone* had copied him now – even the teachers.

But the happiest person in the
whole school was sitting in a corner
all by herself. Nobody was
bothering her –

and she was having
a wonderful time.